THE TORTOISE AND THE DARE

TERRY DEARY'S GREEK TALES

THE TORTOISE AND THE DARE

Illustrated by Helen Flook

A & C Black • London

First published 2007 by
A & C Black Publishers Ltd
38 Soho Square, London, W1D 3HB

www.acblack.com

ISBN 0-7136-8220-5
ISBN 978-0-7136-8220-5

A CIP catalogue for this book is available from the British Library.

This book is produced using paper that is made from wood grown in managed, sustainable forests. It is natural, renewable and recyclable. The logging and manufacturing processes conform to the environmental regulations of the country of origin.

Printed and bound in Great Britain by Bookmarque Ltd, Croydon.

Introduction

Olympia, Greece, 776 BC

Aesop the Greek storyteller said:
Slow and steady wins the race.

It started with the mighty Heracles, the hero of the gods. Heracles won a race at Olympia, the home of the gods. Well, he would win a race – he was the strongest, fastest hero the world has ever known. I think he was like a lot of men. Vain.

"The world must remember my great victory," Heracles said. "Humans must have races every four years! They will be called the Olympics."

The priests said it was a good idea and that's how the games began.

But Heracles didn't just start the Olympic Games ... he started a lot of trouble.

Oh, yes, a lot of people enjoy watching the winners. They love the show, the sport and the excitement. But what about the cheating? What about the arguments?

What about the losers? And what about the women? Women are not allowed to race, of course. They are not even allowed to watch. If they try, they are executed ... thrown off a cliff.

Ooooh! It makes me so angry. I am an angry sort of person. I was angry when I was a girl, all those years ago, and I am still angry when I remember...

I am angry with my brother, Cypselis. *Dear* Cypselis had a bet on a race. And what was the prize? Me! Yes, he bet his own *sister*! Would *you* do that? No, of course not. So do not blame me for being angry now when I tell you the tale of 'The Tortoise and the Dare'.

Chapter One

My brother Cypselis ran in from school, bubbling like a soup pot. He was so happy he didn't notice how miserable the family was.

"The Olympic Games start next week and our head teacher, Master Sophos, said we can have our own school Olympics tomorrow. There will be all sorts of prizes and it'll be more exciting than the real games."

"Nice," I muttered.

"The boys have already started talking about who will win. We're doing the same events as the grown-ups. There's the foot race – 200 paces – then the double foot race – 400 paces. We'll have the standing long jump, quoit throwing and javelin!"

"Great," I said.

"I think I could win the foot race," he babbled. "I'll practise after dinner. What are we having for dinner, Mother? Cheese and milk?"

"Bread and water," she sighed.

"I love cheese and milk!"

"Bread and water," I said, louder.

Cypselis blinked. "An athlete needs cheese and milk."

"Where will we get it from?" I snapped.

Cypselis laughed. "Why, from Nan the goat of course."

Father shook his head. "They came and took Nan away from us."

"Who did?"

"The priests from the temple. They always have a feast when the games start. They will sacrifice 20 goats to Pelops. They took Nan to sacrifice."

"Then what will I eat?" Cypselis wailed.

That's when I lost my temper. "Oh, never mind about poor Nan – who's nearly as old as us. Never mind how Mother and Father will get through the winter. Never mind how we'll find the money for another goat. All you can think about is your own stomach!"

Cypselis blushed. He wasn't really thoughtless, just stupid. He nodded. "Sorry, Ellie," he muttered.

"You deserve to be sacrificed like Pelops*!" I raged.

* As you know, Pelops was the grandson of Zeus. When he was a boy, his father cut him into pieces, stewed his flesh in a pot, and served him as a feast for the gods.

“Maybe I can win us a goat if I win the race,” he said quietly.

I stopped shouting and listened. “A goat is the prize?”

“Not exactly … I had a dare with Big Bacchiad in my class. He said he will give me a goat if I can beat him.”

I frowned. “And what will you give him if *he* beats *you*?” I asked.

Cypselis muttered something.

“What did you say?”

He looked up with a smile as weak as water. “I said he could have you to be his slave, Ellie. I’m sorry! Mother, don’t let her hit me! Mother! Ouch!”

Chapter Two

I know you think I will say I lost my temper again.

I didn't.

I felt sick with fear at what Cypselis had done. When two men make a bargain, then it must be kept. A dare between two boys is just as strong.

Cypselis had bet me against a goat. If he lost the race I would be given away as a slave. There was nothing I could do to stop it now. In Greece, a woman is worthless. A girl is less than worthless*.

Our mother groaned. "Cypselis! Ellie is your twin sister. You shouldn't have risked her like that."

* A Greek teacher called Aristotle had that potty idea – he said that the gods made men to rule the world; women and slaves could not even *think* because they had such weak brains. Women and slaves were just there to do as men told them! Of course Aristotle was a *man*. He *would* say that.

"But I'll *win*," my brother said bravely. "This time tomorrow, we'll have a new goat!"

"But if you *lose*..."

"I won't!"

I stood up. "Let's see you run," I said.

I knew how fast my brother was. We used to race by the river every day when we were young – before Cypselis started school.

He was fast. But I was faster.

We set off across the fields and as fast as he ran, I was still quicker. We climbed a small hill and I reached the top a few paces ahead of him.

The evening sun was low in the sky and the earth was still warm as we lay on the ground, panting.

"You're a tortoise compared to me, Cypselis. A tortoise!"

I looked down into the valley. The stadium stood there with its high banks casting long shadows over the track. Some boys were racing down the course.

"There's Big Bacchiad," Cypselis said, and he pointed at the boy in the lead.

Bacchiad was tall and powerful. He was the son of Olympia's richest farmer and had the strength of one of his father's bulls.

"Let's see how fast he is," I said. I got up and trotted down the hill ahead of Cypselis.

In the stadium, Bacchiad was sweating but pleased with himself. He saw Cypselis and laughed aloud. "I've beaten everyone, Cypselis. And tomorrow I'll beat you."

"You couldn't even beat his sister," I jeered.

The laughter died in Bacchiad's throat. "Who are you to say that?"

"His sister," I said and smiled sweetly.

"My prize," he breathed. "When I win, you will work till you drop." His eyes glittered darkly in his ugly face. "You will rise with the sun and gather wood for the fire. You'll fetch water from the well and cook breakfast. You'll weed in the fields till dark and then..."

"You haven't won me yet," I said. "But I will."

"Like I said, you couldn't even run against me and win. And Cypselis is faster than me," I lied.

Big Bacchiad looked around the group of boys. "Want to see me race a girl?" he said.

They nodded.

"Then you be the starter, Telemachus. We'll race the length of the stadium, turn at the pillar and run back."

"Take your marks..." Telemachus began.

Chapter Three

"Go!" Telemachus cried, and we set off down the track with the low sun in our faces.

Big Bacchiad made the earth shake with his heavy legs. I floated like a butterfly alongside him.

I had speed. But he had strength. We reached the pillar that marked the turning point and we were shoulder to shoulder.

Bacchiad took a step to the side and caught me with his elbow, so he turned first and was five paces ahead of me before I recovered.

I was angry – he brought out the worst of my temper. I made my arms fly like a sparrow's wings and pull me along. I caught up with him before we were halfway down the home stretch.

He saw my shadow alongside him and swayed so he'd barge me aside.

This time I was ready for him. I skipped to his left and passed him on the inside.

There were 30 paces left to run. I had the speed. But did I have the strength? With 20 paces to go, Big Bacchiad was alongside me. He was grunting with the effort. Every pace took him further into the lead and he passed the finish line well ahead.

He sank to the ground, shaking with the pain and forced a grin. "You are quite good, girl. But your brother will have to be better to get near me."

As I walked home with Cypselis, my brother hung his head. "Big Bacchiad beat you ... and you are faster than me. I'll lose."

I smiled. "That's what Bacchiad thinks," I said.

"He beat you."

"I slowed down. I could have beaten him by the length of a goat," I said.

"But you can beat me by the length of two goats. Big Bacchiad will still win tomorrow," Cypselis groaned.

"I know," I said. "You're going to lose."

"Sorry, Ellie. Sorry. I wish there was a way out of it."

"There is..." I said.

Cypselis stopped and looked at me in the half-dark to see if I was joking. "How?"

"Don't race."

"If I refuse to race, he'll claim you as the prize anyway," my brother sighed.

"*I* will race him," I said simply. "We are twins. Tonight I will get Mother to take the shears to my hair and cut it as short as yours. No one will be able to tell us apart!"

"You're proud of your hair, Elena," he said. "You'd give it up for me?"

"No," I snapped. "I'll be giving it up for my freedom. Now, let's get home and start cutting."

Chapter Four

The school Olympics were set to start in the morning, before the day grew too hot. Every boy and master in the school was there as well as some of the boys' fathers.

Some young men from the real Olympics were there. Their muscles were shiny and as hard as brass, and they strutted like cockerels to their seats by the finish line – the best seats.

There were no women there, of course ... I was dressed in Cypselis's tunic and my short hair felt odd.

Big Bacchiad looked at me. "Hello, Cypselis," he sneered. His fat face was bulging as he chewed on some leaves. I hadn't eaten breakfast. We had no goat, no food.

Big Bacchiad didn't suspect a thing. My twin brother wore a hood so no one would see the switch and walked with me into the arena. "Watch out for him at the turn – he'll try to barge you out wide."

I kept my temper. "I know, Cypselis. I raced against him last night, remember. I'll be watching out for it. Anyway, I may be ahead of him at the pillar and he won't be able to elbow me."

"The other boys may get in your way – some of them are very fast, but only Big Bacchiad can keep going the full distance."

"And me," I said.

"And you," Cypselis said.

The head teacher, Master Sophos, marched onto the starters' platform and clapped his hands. Everyone fell silent.

"Welcome to the school Olympics. Remember, these games must be played in the spirit of the real Olympics. The most important thing in the Olympic Games is not winning but taking part; the great thing is not winning but fighting well. Let us have no cheating, boys!" He nodded to the bronzed men in the stands. "Let us show our heroes that we too can be heroes! May the best man win!"

Or the best girl, I smirked.

The crowd cheered and the athletes began to sort themselves out into groups – the javelin throwers at one end of the track and the runners near the start.

Master Sophus turned to us and smiled. "Now, boys, take off your clothes!"

The boys started to slip their tunics over their heads.

I turned to Cypselis. "Why are they taking their clothes off?"

"The Olympics are always run without clothes. Didn't you know?"

"How *could* I know?" I hissed. "Girls aren't allowed to watch the games, are they, you stupid, *stupid* boy!"

"They won't let you run in a tunic," my brother shrugged.

"Well I can't take it off or they'll know I'm not a boy. Didn't you think of that?"

He just shrugged again. "I thought you knew. I thought you'd come up with a way round the problem."

For once in my life even my wild temper couldn't find any words to answer him.

I tore Cypselis's hood and tunic off him and quickly put the hood over my head.

"Run, tortoise, run," I whispered. Then I hurried off to find a seat in the stands.

Chapter Five

My brother tried. At the turn he was level with Big Bacchiad. The rest of the runners were already lengths behind.

The big boy leaned towards Cypselis and aimed to hit him with his shoulder. Cypselis skipped aside and Bacchiad missed. He stumbled and went round the turn with his arms whirling, trying to keep his balance.

By the time they were halfway to the finish, Cypselis was lengths ahead but his head was rolling from side to side. I knew it meant he was exhausted. His legs were shaking and his ankles looked weak.

I thought I could hear Bacchiad's pounding feet even from the stands and even above the shouts of the crowd. Every stride took him closer to Cypselis. Every step took Cypselis closer to the finishing line. My tortoise brother had never run so bravely. Tears filled my eyes and I screamed his name till my throat was raw.

But his weary legs stumbled and Bacchiad pounded past him just before they reached the finish line.

A man in a rich cloak ran from the stands and wrapped his arms around the big boy.

He pushed some leaves into his hands and Bacchiad chewed on them hungrily. The man was Bacchiad's father and he raised his son's arms above his head in victory as Cypselis sank to his knees in despair.

I left the stand and walked over to my brother. I wrapped an arm around him just as Master Sophos stepped down from the starters' platform.

Bacchiad's father was grinning like a wolf. He reached out a hand to take the winner's crown of celery leaves from the head teacher.

But Master Sophos spoke sharply. "You have just given your son some plant to eat. He was eating it before the race, too."

"Celery," the father said.

Master Sophos stretched out a hand and took a piece from Bacchiad's hand. He rubbed it and sniffed at the juice he'd squeezed out. "It is not celery. It is the candlewort plant."

"So?"

"So ... athletes know that eating candlewort makes you run faster for a while. It is banned. It is cheating."

"There's no harm in it!" the father huffed.

"The most important thing in the Olympic Games is not winning but fighting well. Bacchiad has run an unfair race. He did not fight well." The head teacher stepped back onto the platform and held up a hand for silence. "Bacchiad has cheated. Bacchiad loses the race. I declare the winner to be Cypselis!"

My brother looked in wonder as the wreath was placed on his forehead. The crowd cheered till their throats were as sore as mine.

That night, my brother showed Father the winner's crown. Boys and men. Easily pleased.

And me? I showed my mother something far more precious.

The goat. That night we ate well. Mother raised a glass of milk in a toast to us. "Remember, children, the great thing in life is not inning but *eating* well!"

THE BOY WHO CRIED HORSE

TROY, 1180 BC

Acheron is the best liar in Troy. In his stories he can make King Paris and the Trojan heroes sound like gods. When a stranger arrives in the city, with news that the Greek enemy have left without a fight, Acheron is suspicious. But will anyone believe his latest story?

Greek Tales are exciting, funny stories based on historical events – short chapters and illustrations throughout are perfect for building reading confidence.

ISBN 978 0 7136 8216 8 £4.99

THE TOWN MOUSE AND THE SPARTAN HOUSE

ATHENS, GREECE, 430 BC

Athens is at war with Sparta, home to the cruellest people on Earth. But when plague spreads through the city, Darius is forced to leave and join his uncle, a Spartan general. To the Spartans, Darius is as worthless as a mouse. How can he prove them wrong?

Greek Tales are exciting, funny stories based on historical events – short chapters and illustrations throughout are perfect for building reading confidence.

ISBN 978 0 7136 8221 2 £4.99

SYRACUSE, GREECE, 213 BC

Archimedes is the cleverest man in Greece. So when the Romans attack, everyone believes he'll find a way to save them. Lydia, his slave, thinks so, too, and cheers with the crowd as he creates one amazing invention after another. But who is the *real* brains behind them all?

Greek Tales are exciting, funny stories based on historical events – short chapters and illustrations throughout are perfect for building reading confidence.

ISBN 978 0 7136 8222 9 £4.99